To Josh and
Gabrielle
with love from
Aunt Cathy

Because I Love You So Much
A Treasury of Stories for Sharing
This edition produced 2006 for
Advanced Marketing Services, Inc.
5880 Oberlin Drive, Suite 400, San Diego,
California 92121 9653 by
LITTLE TIGER PRESS
An imprint of Magi Publications
1 The Coda Centre, 189 Munster Road,
London SW6 6AW, UK
www.littletigerpress.com

Just For You!
Christine Leeson
Illustrated by Andy Ellis
First published in Great Britain
2004 by Little Tiger Press,
an imprint of Magi Publications
Text copyright
© Christine Leeson 2004
Illustrations copyright
© Andy Ellis 2004

Oops-a-Daisy!
Claire Freedman
Illustrated by Gaby Hansen
First published in Great Britain 2004
by Little Tiger Press,
an imprint of Magi Publications
Text copyright © Claire Freedman 2004
Illustrations copyright
© Gaby Hansen 2004

One Magical Morning
Claire Freedman
Illustrated by Louise Ho
First published in Great Britain 2005
by Little Tiger Press,
an imprint of Magi Publications
Text copyright
© Claire Freedman 2005
Illustrations copyright
© Louise Ho 2005

Don't Be Afraid, Little Foal
Caroline Pitcher
Illustrated by Jane Chapman
First published in Great Britain 1998
by Little Tiger Press,
an imprint of Magi Publications
Text copyright © Caroline Pitcher 1998
Illustrations copyright
© Jane Chapman 1998

By My Side, Little Panda
Claire Freedman
Illustrated by Rory Tyger
First published in Great Britain 2004
by Little Tiger Press,
an imprint of Magi Publications
Text copyright
© Claire Freedman 2004
Illustrations copyright
© Rory Tyger 2004

Love Like This
Peter Kavanagh
Illustrated by Jane Chapman
First published in Great Britain 2002
by Little Tiger Press,
an imprint of Magi Publications
Text copyright © Peter Kavanagh 2002
Illustrations copyright
© Jane Chapman 2002

Because
I Love
You So
Much

A Treasury of Stories for Sharing

LITTLE TIGER PRESS

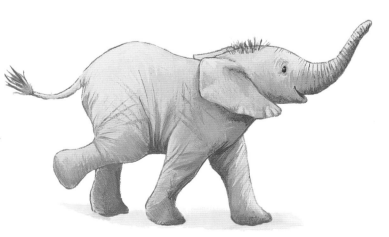

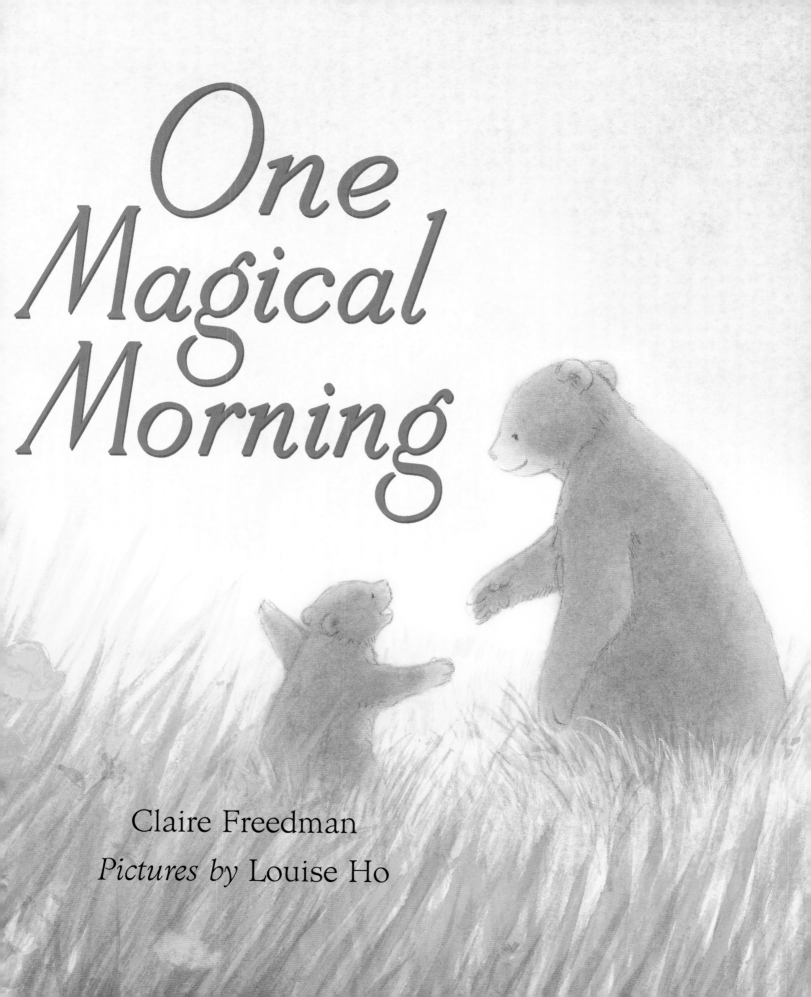

One Magical Morning

Claire Freedman

Pictures by Louise Ho

In the shadowy woods,
one clear summer's morning,
Mommy took Little Bear
to see the day dawning.

The bears walked together
through grass drenched with dew.
Little Bear skipped,
as little bears do.

Little Bear gazed
as the sunrise unfurled.
"Up here," he cried,
"you can see the whole world!"

As the silvery moon faded
high in the sky,
Twinkle-eyed voles
came scurrying by.

And a little mouse gazed
as the morning sun
Melted the stars away,
one by one.

Fox cubs played while
the mist swirled like smoke,
Wrapping the trees
in its wispy cloak.

A pigeon coo-cooed
from a branch way up high.
Little Bear laughed,
"Look at me! Watch me fly!"

They stopped for a drink
at a babbling stream,
And the sun turned the forest
soft pink, gold and green.

Bushy-tailed squirrels
scampered down trees,
Hunting for pine cones
hidden by leaves.

27

"Look, Mommy!" cried
Little Bear in delight,
As a mole burst, blinking,
into the light.

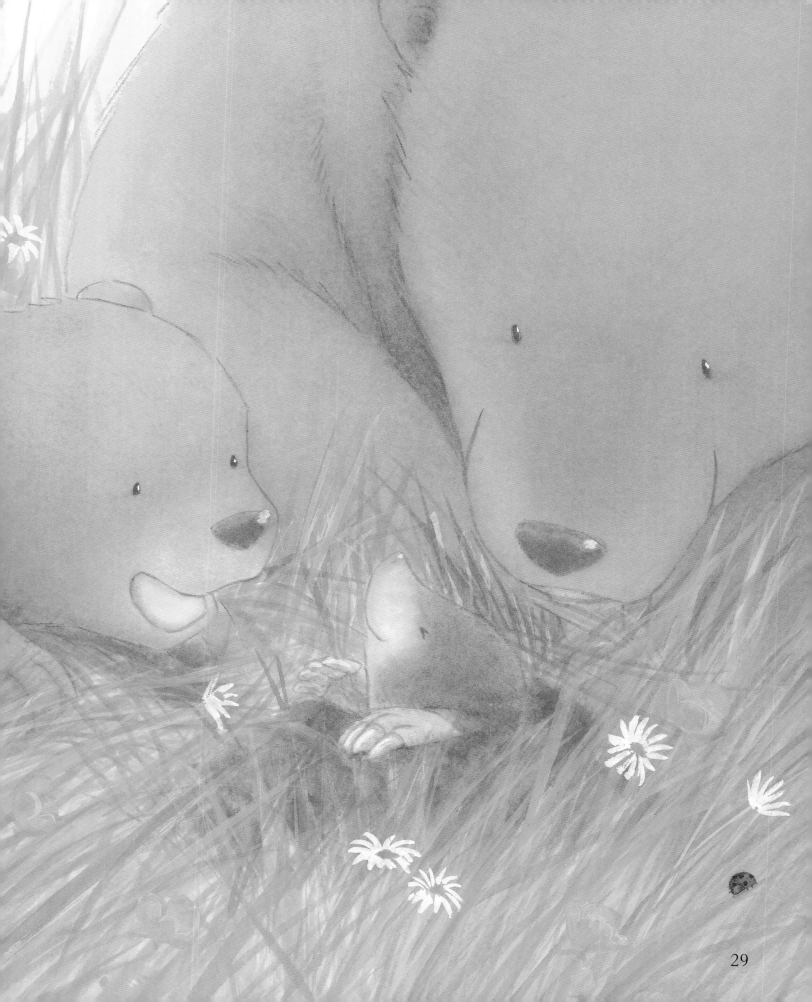

Mommy Bear smiled,
"Over here, take a peep!"
Bear's friend, Little Rabbit,
lay curled up asleep.

"Wake up, Little Rabbit,
come and play in the sun.
It's a beautiful day –
and it's just begun!"

33

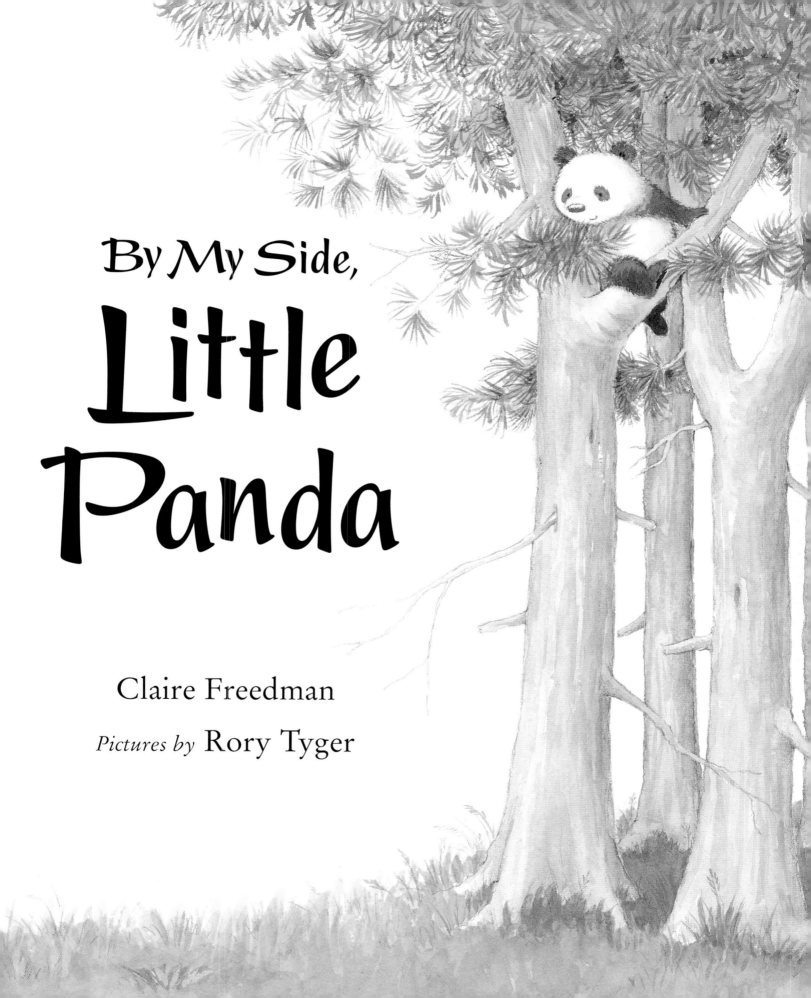

By My Side, Little Panda

Claire Freedman

Pictures by Rory Tyger

Little Panda and his mother did everything together.
Together they explored the mountain tops,
where the snow lay too deep to melt.

Together they splashed in icy streams,
startling tiny, shiny fish . . .

and rolled down grassy slopes,
carpeted with early spring flowers.

And as the first stars twinkled above
the snowy crags, they were still together,
snuggled up, cozy and warm.

"The world is full of wonders for
a brave little panda like you,"
said Mother Panda. "You'll discover
echoing caves where butterflies hide.
You'll play in sparkling waterfalls,
and climb trees so high you'll almost
touch the clouds!"

"Will I really do all that?" asked
Little Panda.

"One day!" Mother Panda said.

And soon Little Panda was asleep,
dreaming of dancing butterflies!

Springtime passed by and the days became warmer. Little Panda was growing bigger every day.

One morning, when the sun shone and summer was in the air, Little Panda asked, "What should we do today?"

"Why don't you play in the meadow?" his mother said. "You could splash in the stream."

"On my own?" said Little Panda. "Without you?"

"We could go to the Great Pine Forest, if you'd prefer," Mother Panda said.

"Together?" Little Panda asked.

"Together!" his mother replied.

Little Panda had never been in the
Great Pine Forest before.

Golden monkeys with bright blue
faces leapt through the leafy trees.
Soft gray deer peered out from misty
shadows and colorful birds fluttered
across their path.

"Look, Mommy, look!" Little
Panda cried, his eyes shining
with excitement.

Deeper in the forest, Mother Panda paused.
"This is the sweetest, juiciest bamboo on
the whole mountain!"she said. "Want to
climb this tree and pick some?"

"But it's so tall!" gasped Little Panda.

"Don't worry. I'll be right beside you,"
his mother assured him.

The two pandas
climbed to the top
of the swaying tree.
  "I'm good at
climbing, aren't I?"
Little Panda said.
  "Very good!"
his mother agreed.

They sat in the branches and munched and crunched on the best bamboo Little Panda had ever tasted!

"I've seen many new things today," Little Panda said. "The forest is big and exciting!"

"I know," Mother Panda said. "You're going to have lots of fun exploring it all!"

The next day, the two bears walked down to the Great Pine Forest again.

Little Panda heard a rustling sound in the trees. A young panda played peek-a-boo with him through the leaves. Little Panda laughed!

"Would you like to play with him?" asked Mother Panda.

Little Panda hesitated . . . .

"I'll be here if you need me!" she said.

The friendly panda poked his head through the leaves again! Little Panda clambered up through the branches to join him.

Little Panda and his new friend chased
each other through the tall trees and played
hide-and-seek in the thick bamboo.

They raced to the stream
and splashed in the cool water.

They rolled dry and relaxed in
the grass together. Little Panda
had the best day!

But soon, Little Panda heard his
mother calling him.

"Time to go home!"

"Already?" Little Panda cried,
scrambling back through the trees.

"We'll come again tomorrow!"
Mother Panda said.

Mother Panda and Little Panda headed back
up the mountain.

"Did you have fun with your new
friend today?" she asked him.

"Oh, yes!" cried Little Panda happily,
bouncing over the rocks. "We chased
each other through the forest! We climbed
the biggest tree you've ever seen!"

Little Panda gazed out across the valley, glowing pink under the setting sun.

"Tomorrow I'm going to explore all the way to the Big River!" he told his mother sleepily.

Mother Panda smiled as she wrapped her arms
around Little Panda. He closed his eyes and
snuggled deep into her warm fur.

The stars began to twinkle in the darkening sky.
But Little Panda didn't see them. He was fast asleep!

JUST FOR YOU!

Christine Leeson

Pictures by Andy Ellis

Jenny opened her eyes. It was a sweet summer morning and it was so early the sun was barely up.

"Wake up," Jenny whispered to her brothers and sister. "It's Mom's birthday today. We have to wrap her present."

All the mice jumped out of bed.

"I'll help!" cried Jenny's sister excitedly.

"I'll help, too!"

"And me!"

Jenny stepped back as the
mice pushed forward. "Be careful!"
she cried. "You'll break...!"

SMASH!

It was too late. The present was pulled from Jenny's paws and shattered on the ground.

"Oh no," said Jenny, looking at the broken gift. "Maybe we can find something else before Mom wakes up. Come on, everybody!"

The mice scampered outside. Overhead, the sky was still flushed with the pink sunrise.

"This way," called Jenny, but her older brother had already seen something in the shadows.

"Look, look!" he shouted. "How about these?"
Next to the path there was a cluster of juicy
red strawberries.

"*M*m, what a treat!" Jenny said, licking
her lips. "Mom will love them!"

At that moment Vole scurried out of the dewy grass.

"Thank you," she said. "You've found my strawberries. I was carrying some home for my family's breakfast when I dropped a few. I've really got my paws full here!"

"Oh," said Jenny, feeling disappointed. "We thought we'd found a present for our mother."

"Maybe she'd like something
else instead," said Vole. "How
about those?" She nodded toward
some feathers caught between two
branches of a nearby bush.

"Oh yes! They'll make a lovely soft pillow!" said Jenny, and she scampered off to gather them. "Mom will be so surprised. This is going to be the best birthday present ever!"

But just then Bluejay chirped from above, "My feathers! Thank goodness you've found them. I need them to line my nest and keep my eggs warm."

"You'd better take them then," said Jenny. "They would have made a nice present for our mother's birthday, though."

Bluejay thought for a moment.
"Does your mother like flowers?" she asked.
"I can see a nice one in the grass just
over there."

"Oh thank you!" cried Jenny, and the
mice scurried off as fast as they could.

The grass was very tall and the little
mice had to push and scramble through
it in search of the flower.

"I can't see it anywhere," cried Jenny.

"I see it!" shouted her little brother.
"Quick, Jenny! Over here!"

He picked up a large
white daisy and waved it
over his head. "Do you
think Mom will like it?"
he asked, stumbling under
the flower's weight.

"She'll love it!"
Jenny said. "It will
make a beautiful
present! Let's hurry
back home before
she wakes up."

Just then Rabbit hopped over. "Wait, wait!" he called. "That's my flower! My grandma's not feeling well and I was going to take it home for her. I put it down for a minute and then it was gone."

"Oh, we're sorry," said Jenny. "You should take it for her. We can find another present for our mother."

"Thank you, little mice," said Rabbit as he hopped away. "I hope you find something soon."

Jenny scratched her head. The sun was climbing over the trees into the deep blue sky. Their mother would be waking up soon and they still hadn't found a birthday present.

Suddenly something fluttered across the path. Jenny leaped up and grabbed it…

but it was only a piece of paper, not nearly pretty enough for a present.

"We'll never find anything! Mom's birthday will be ruined!" Jenny burst out. The mice began to cry. Big tears plopped down onto the back of the paper.

"Stop," sniffed Jenny. "We're making it all sticky."

Then she suddenly had an idea. "Wait here!" Jenny squeaked. "I'll be back in a minute."

Jenny raced off to find Vole, Bluejay, and Rabbit. They were happy to share a little bit of the things they had found that morning, and soon Jenny's arms were full as she ran back to her brothers and sister. They squeaked with excitement as Jenny told them her plan.

Soon they were all busy, shredding and sticking, until at
last the present was ready. The little mice ran home.

"Wake up, Mom! Happy birthday!" they giggled. "We've got a present just for you!"

Mother Mouse looked at the picture her children had made. It was red with strawberry, blue with feathers, and sprinkled golden with flower pollen.

"It's beautiful," she smiled, and hugged her mice close. "Thank you, everyone. It's the best birthday present ever."

Oops-a-Daisy!

Claire Freedman

Pictures by
Gaby Hansen

There was a lot of jumping and thumping over
in the meadow. Mama Rabbit was teaching
Daisy how to hop.

  "I'm going to try hopping all by myself!"
Daisy cried excitedly. "Watch me, Mama!"

  Daisy took a huge leap,
lost her balance, and fell
over backward!

"Never mind!" said
Mama Rabbit. "Try again."
So Daisy did . . .

hippity-hoppity flop!

hoppity-floppity whoops!

"I don't think I can do it, Mama!"
Daisy cried.

"No one gets it right first time,"
said Mama Rabbit, picking up Daisy
and dusting her off. "Look at Little
Mouse over by the duck pond."

Mama Mouse was showing Little Mouse
how to climb the reeds to reach
the golden seed at the top.

Little Mouse inched closer
and closer to the top. She had
almost reached the seeds when . . .

slippity-zippity!

Little Mouse slid down again with a bump!
"Learning new things can be hard for
everyone!" Daisy said.

Daisy decided to practice little bunny hops.
"Stay in a straight line," Mama Rabbit
called. "That's it!"

Up down, up down wobbled Daisy
through the tall grass.
"Hooray, I can do it!"
she cried. "Small hops
are easier!"

Daisy saw a
big molehill ahead.
She jumped a huge jump . . .

whoopsity-oopsity!

"Ouch! Who put that prickly thistle there?"
Daisy said. "And why won't my
feet do what I tell
them to?"

"They will, in time!" said Mama. She picked up
Daisy and gave her a hug. "Have you seen the
mess Little Badger is making?"

Little Badger was out in the field,
learning how to dig tunnels . . .

crashity-smashity!

Another one of his tunnels collapsed.
Little Badger and Daddy Badger were
getting muddier and muddier!
"I'm glad I'm not the only one who
needs more practice," giggled Daisy.

Daisy and Mama Rabbit rested by the duck pond.
Blue-green dragonflies darted around them
whizzily-busily.

"Ribbit!" A big frog hopped out
through the tall grass.

"I wish I could jump like
that!" said Daisy. "Do you
think I ever will?"

"You'll jump even higher!"
Mama replied.

"Really?" cried Daisy,
leaping up. "I'll try
some more!"

"One, two . . . one, two," counted
Daisy as she bounced. "Whee,
look at me! Hopping is fun!"
"That's much better," Mama
Rabbit called. "Oh no! Watch out, Daisy!" . . .

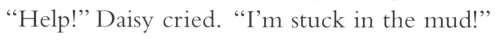

bumpity-thumpity!

Daisy slithered down the slippery bank and skidded into the pond!

"Ribbit, ribbit!" croaked the frog in surprise.

"Help!" Daisy cried. "I'm stuck in the mud!"

Mama Rabbit ran down and pulled Daisy free.
"I was so busy counting that I didn't see
the pond," sighed Daisy. "There's so much
to remember all at once!"

"Cheer up, Daisy," Mama Rabbit said. "Let's practice together."
Paw in paw, Daisy and Mama Rabbit hopped and skipped
around the duck pond.

Little Duckling was out on the water,
practicing his swimming.

"Little Duckling isn't doing very well,"
said Daisy. "He can only swim
in tiny circles!"

Then suddenly . . .

splashity-crashity!

Little Duckling sailed right into some water lilies! Quickly his mother swam across to untangle him.

"There's someone else who didn't look where they were going!" Mama Rabbit smiled.

Daisy laughed. "I'm going to try hopping by myself one more time!" she said.

Up down, up down bounced Daisy.
Wibbly-wobbly, hippity-hoppity hop!
"That's it!" cried Mama. "Keep going!"
"Did you see how high I jumped?" called Daisy proudly.
"I was almost flying! I can do it, Mama! I can do it!"
"Well done, Daisy!" said Mama Rabbit. "You're hopping!"

Daisy hopped . . .

 and skipped . . .

and jumped.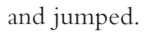

114

At last her legs were too tired to keep hopping!
"I'll have to carry you home this evening!"
Mama laughed.

Happily, Daisy climbed into Mama Rabbit's arms and buried herself snuggly-huggly into her soft warm fur.
"Do you think Little Mouse, Little Badger, and Little Duckling learned how to climb and dig and swim?" Daisy asked Mama sleepily.

"I'm sure they did!"
Mama Rabbit whispered.
"In the end!"

Don't Be Afraid, Little Foal

CAROLINE PITCHER

PICTURES BY
JANE CHAPMAN

One moonlit night, while the wind raged and the
rain drummed on the stable roof, a foal was born.
His mother the mare breathed on him softly until
he struggled up on a tangle of long legs.

"What's that noise?" asked the foal.
"Just the wind blowing in the hills," answered the mare. "When you are big and your legs aren't wobbly anymore, you will run with the wind over the hills."
"Will you be there with me?" asked the foal.
"No," said his mother. "But you won't think of me then."

125

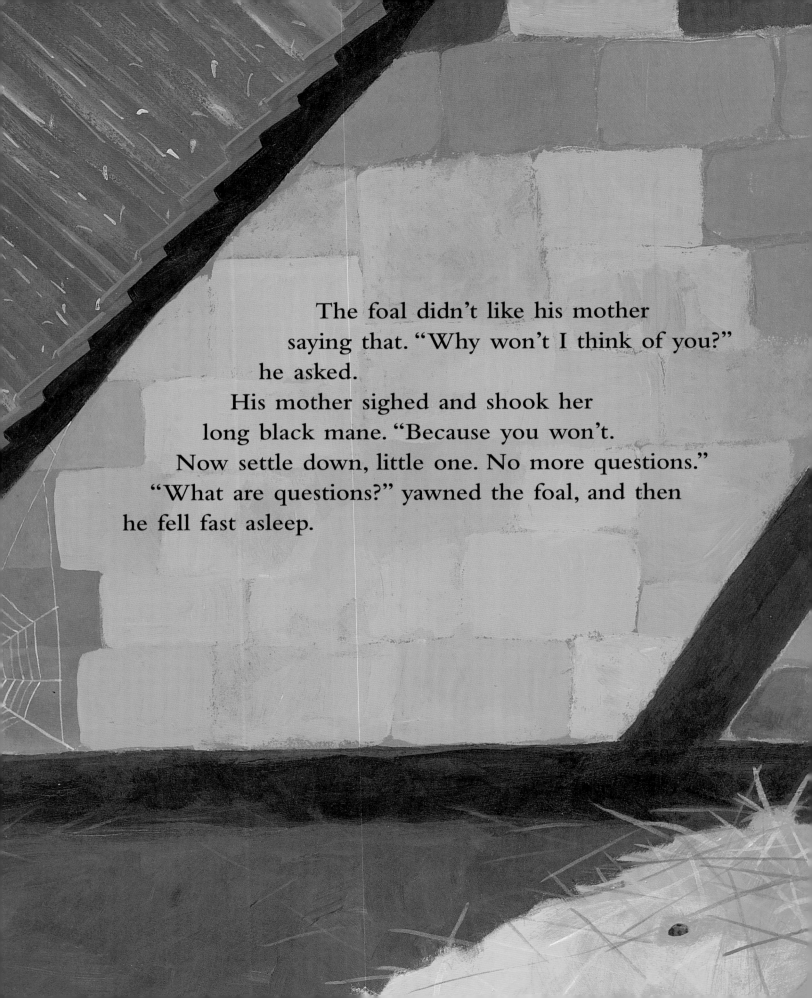

The foal didn't like his mother
saying that. "Why won't I think of you?"
he asked.
His mother sighed and shook her
long black mane. "Because you won't.
Now settle down, little one. No more questions."
"What are questions?" yawned the foal, and then
he fell fast asleep.

Spring came, and the foal's
legs grew longer and stronger
so that his head just reached
the top of the stable door.
"What's outside?" he asked.
"It's a field," said the mare.
"Soon you will be able to go
there with me and run all the
way around and back again."
"I don't think I want to,"
said the foal, drawing back.
"I don't like Outside. I like
it here."

The foal's legs grew even stronger
and longer. Now he could see right
over the stable door. He saw other horses.
There was a great shire horse with giant
hooves, and a tiny Shetland pony with very
long hair. He saw a horse as dark as the
night sky, and a pony as pale as moonlight.

"Where are their mothers?" he asked.
"Some of them are here and some are at
other stables," said the mare. "They give
people rides. I'll soon do that, too,
little one, while you stay behind."
Stay behind!
"No," said the foal, turning his back.
"I don't want to think about it."

When the days grew warmer,
the mare and her foal went out
into the field. They ran all the
way around it and back again.

Twilight fell, and the foal became uneasy.

"Can't we go back to the stable now?" he asked.

"No," said his mother. "When the nights are warm, we stay outside."

"But it's *dark*!"

"It's dark in the stable, too, little one. It's the same dark."

"It's not such a big dark there," said the foal.

"I can't see you out here when you move away from me. I'm all alone."

"You know I'm here, even if you can't see me," whispered the mare.

The foal lifted his head
in the darkness. "What's
making that noise?" he asked.
"Just the wind. Don't you
remember hearing it when
you were very small?"
"Yes," said the foal. "But where
is it?"
"You know it's there, but you
can't see it."
"Just like you in the dark,
Mom," he whispered.

One morning, the foal woke late. But where was his mother? The foal looked inside the stable, but she wasn't there. Then he saw her by the fence. She had a bridle over her head and a saddle on her back.

"I'm going back to work," she called to him. "I'm going to give rides again.

"And who will ride me?" cried the foal with excitement.

"You're too little to be ridden yet," explained his mother.

"Your back is weak, your mouth is soft as silk, and your legs would snap like twigs."

"But I'll be all alone," he wailed. "Oh, please stay with me!"

"No," said the mare as a little girl climbed onto her back. "You'll be just fine."
The foal watched as his mother and her rider trotted out of sight. He was all alone.
"Come back, Mom!" he neighed, and his voice echoed in the hills.

He heard something answer him, but it wasn't his mother. It was the wind! The wind had come down from the hills to play with him. It blew in his mane and his tail, and it blew in the trees and stirred all the leaves. It blew a butterfly for the foal to chase, and it blew a path in the meadow that he could run right through. It even blew waves in the water of his drinking trough.

The foal jumped and ran and bucked and chased and flicked his little black tail. He ran with the wind all morning.

And then, just as the foal was too tired to run and jump anymore, his mother came back. She nuzzled his neck and said, "You see—nothing bad happened to you when you were alone."

Oh my, thought the foal. I was having so much fun I didn't think of Mom once.

"I wasn't alone," he said. "The wind played with me."

"So you didn't think of me at all?"

"Well, maybe a *little* bit," said the foal.

"That's good," said the mare. "I was thinking of you the whole time!

Love
Like
This

PETER KAVANAGH

PICTURES BY

JANE CHAPMAN

The pale sun rises through morning mist.
I love my mama on days like this.

When storm winds blow,
we shelter together. Nothing can
harm us while we have each other.

Later we chase across hot dusty plains,
stomping and stamping and playing new games.

154

When the bright sun rises
hotter and higher, we stride along
by the cool fast river.

The water is clean and we're covered in dust. We jump in together and let it wash over us.

We dip and dive and splash and splish.
Fun like this is all we could wish.

We walk in the grass to dry in the sun
and sing together in trumpeting fun.

Sometimes we laugh for no reason at all,
comparing our trunks, one big, one small.

We gaze at the birds flying into the night
and the stars in the sky, all twinkly and bright.

And when we lie in the soft dewy grass,
you tell me elephant tales from the past.

Last thing at night we curl in a hug,
safe and happy, cozy and snug.

And we sink into sleep and dream of new days.
Love like this is love always.